Will the REAL SANTA Please Stand Up?

Peggy Mason and Linda Marie

So, you believe in Santa Claus
A man all dressed in red.
Who goes from house to house at night,
While children are in bed.

Will the REAL SANTA Please Stand Up?

ISBN 978-1-64670-417-0 (Paperback)
ISBN 978-1-64670-418-7 (Hardcover)
ISBN 978-1-64670-419-4 (Digital)

Covenant Books
11661 Hwy 707
Murrells Inlet, SC 29576
www.covenantbooks.com

Who rings his bell for charity.
Who asks if you've been good.

Do you believe in Santa Claus?
Maybe it's time you should.

A child's dreams are shattered,
When Santa's declared *'untrue'*!

But his little heart holds tight,
To a tiny bit of truth.

7

Someone was that Santa Claus,
That man all dressed in red.

So please don't try to tell me,
That Santa Claus is dead.

He stood outside the market,
When it was bitter cold.
Mama gave him money,
And he said her heart was gold.

Once while sitting in a chair,

I watched as people stopped to stare.
HOMELESS
VETERAN
ANYTHING HELPS
BLESS YOU

14

And with friends beneath our light,
He sang of peace and silent night.

STOP

Is it so hard to see he's true?
Don't you see, it starts with *you*?
An extra smile, a helping hand.
A song of peace, good will toward man.
A *real* Santa knows,
These things are just a start.
A *real* Santa's not a who,
But a feeling in your heart.

When people stop believing,
And the twinkle leaves their eye,
When giving means receiving,
And love is just a lie,

When snow is just to shovel,
And crowds are just to push,

Not only has Christ left Christmas,
But so has the Santa in all of us.

The End

About the Authors

The Marie Sisters & Co. is a group of five sisters who all have the middle name Marie. They were named for polkas and waltzes, and their dad hoped some day they would become like the Lennon Sisters. While they've been known to sing and play with their dad in a polka band, they also come together to support a good cause. They are often joined by their many family members as well as extended family and friends.

The Marie Sisters were raised to believe that family is forever, and good friends are often considered family. Linda Marie is the second oldest of the sisters and has always dreamed of writing children's books. A lifelong career in early education, a spirited childhood, and a vivid imagination provide an abundance of experience and memories for an intriguing selection of storytelling material.

Peggy Mason is the youngest of four girls growing up in a rural community. She received an associate degree in early childhood education and has worked with children, families, and communities throughout her career. In 2016, she moved to Florida with her husband Mark and two dogs and currently works with special needs children. Working with children, she has come to appreciate their innocence, imagination, and eagerness to learn about the world around them.